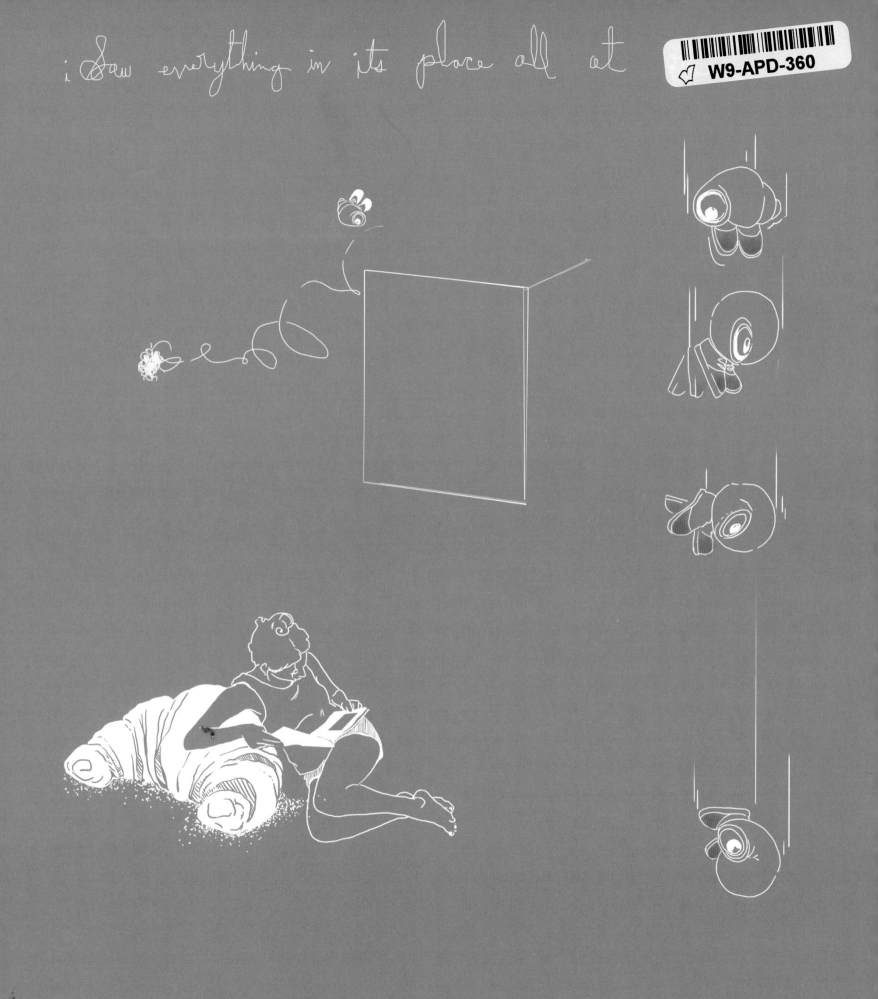

A division of Penguin Young Readers Group
Published by the Penguin Group
Penguin Group (USA) LLC
345 Hudson Street
New York, New York 10014

USA / Canada / UK / Ireland / Australia / New Zealand / India / South Africa / China
Penguin.com
A Penguin Random House Company

ISBN: 978-1-59514-456-0

Printed in China

1 3 5 7 9 10 8 6 4 2

Images by Dean Fleischer-Camp
Painted by Amy Lind

Marcel the Shell

The Most Surprised I've Ever Been

By Dean Fleischer-Camp & Jenny Slate

razOr
bill

AN IMPRINT OF PENGUIN GROUP (USA) LLC

These are my shoes.

This is my face.

This is me, Marcel.

I'm feeling pretty good about that.

One thing about a new
day—you absolutely never
know where it will go. Even
if you know where it starts.

Usually in the morning,
I get out of my bread and
start my day. I don't read
the newspaper because it
turns my shoes black.

And I can't have the coffee
because one time I took half
a sip and I didn't blink for
five hours.

But that's not the surprise
I wanted to tell you about.
I wanted to tell you about the
day I got the most surprised.

I remember how the day
began. I was walking on
the blanket with Alan and
thinking about how much
I love cake.

I'm not exactly sure what
happened next. All I
remember is this:

 **I am walking on the blanket.**

2.

I am sailing through the cool
morning air 200cm off the ground.

Sometimes, when something truly surprising happens,
it feels like it lasts a long time, even if it really doesn't.

I was probably only up there for a few seconds, but it felt like much more.

Everything looked so small.

I could see the whole rug and
all of its far-flung fringes.

I could see the tennis sneaker.
But I could not smell its stink.

I even saw the baby.

He didn't seem to be the
beast that the local news
warned us about. He just
seemed sleepy and fat.

I don't know why they
put him in the jail.

I saw my grandmother's
house. Even from such
a tall, strange height, it
made me feel the way it
always makes me feel:
happy, sweet & safe.

Her name is Nana Connie.
She has one of those big,
old-fashioned breads.
It's French!

I felt the wind on my
shell, and I thought about
her journey when she
was my age.

Her family traveled here by coat pocket. That's actually where she met my grandfather, who was handsome & dashing & good.

She still sleeps on the left side of the bread.

I thought about my own
bread and how it's just
a plain white square.

My Nana reminds me
that sometimes things
should be beautiful just
to be beautiful.

And then, suddenly, I
couldn't go any higher.
I felt weightless, and
for a second, I think I
stopped moving.

I thought about how
astronauts do this as
a job. They go up there
just to look around
and tell us about that.

I saw everything in its place all at once.

It was the quietest quiet I've ever heard.

And before I
could take it all in,
I started to fall
back down.

The world beneath
me was getting
bigger and bigger.
My shell made a
whistling noise.
*I've never heard
that before,*
I thought.

I was scared.

I thought about
the other times
I've been surprised
and didn't know
what to do.

One time an airplane crashed
on the rug. Luckily, nobody
was aboard. They think that's
why it crashed.

One time I was babysitting and
the baby said its first word. Its
first word was "macaroni."

And another time a popcorn
went off right in front of
my face!

But this time…

took the cake.

So all of that—the suddenly and the sailing and the seeing and the whistling and the falling—that was the most surprised I've ever been.

And as quickly as it started, the whistling stopped, and I stopped, and the rest of the day began.

Special thanks: Janet